Rapunzel

First printing

PUBLISHED BY WINSTON-DEREK PUBLISHERS, INC.
Nashville, Tennessee 37205

Library of Congress Catalog Card No: 90-71854
ISBN: 1-55523-408-9

Printed in the United States of America

For Nina

THEY NAMED THE BABY RAPUNZEL

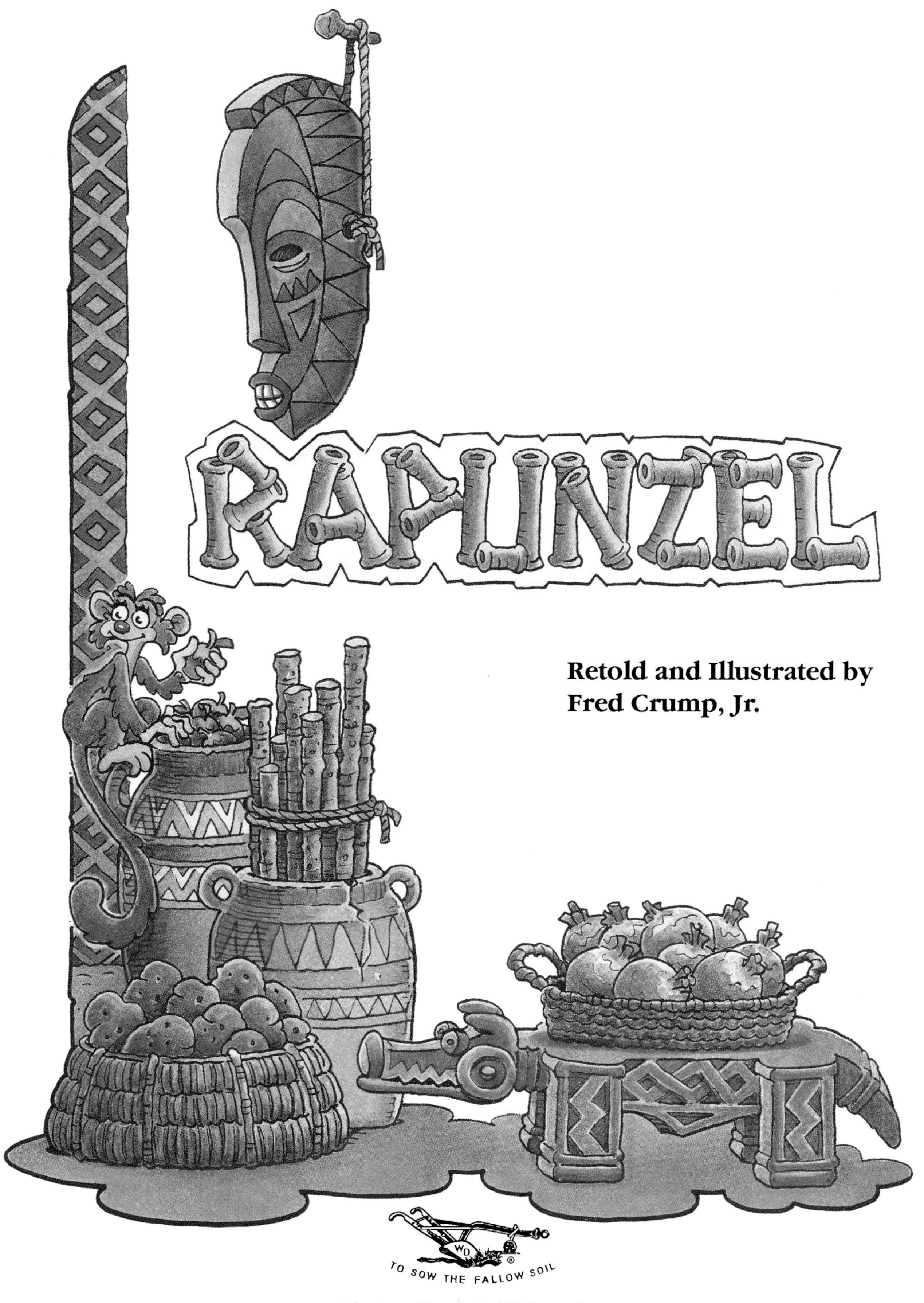

RAPUNZEL

Retold and Illustrated by
Fred Crump, Jr.

Winston-Derek Publishers, Inc.
Pennywell Drive—P.O. Box 90883
Nashville, TN 37209

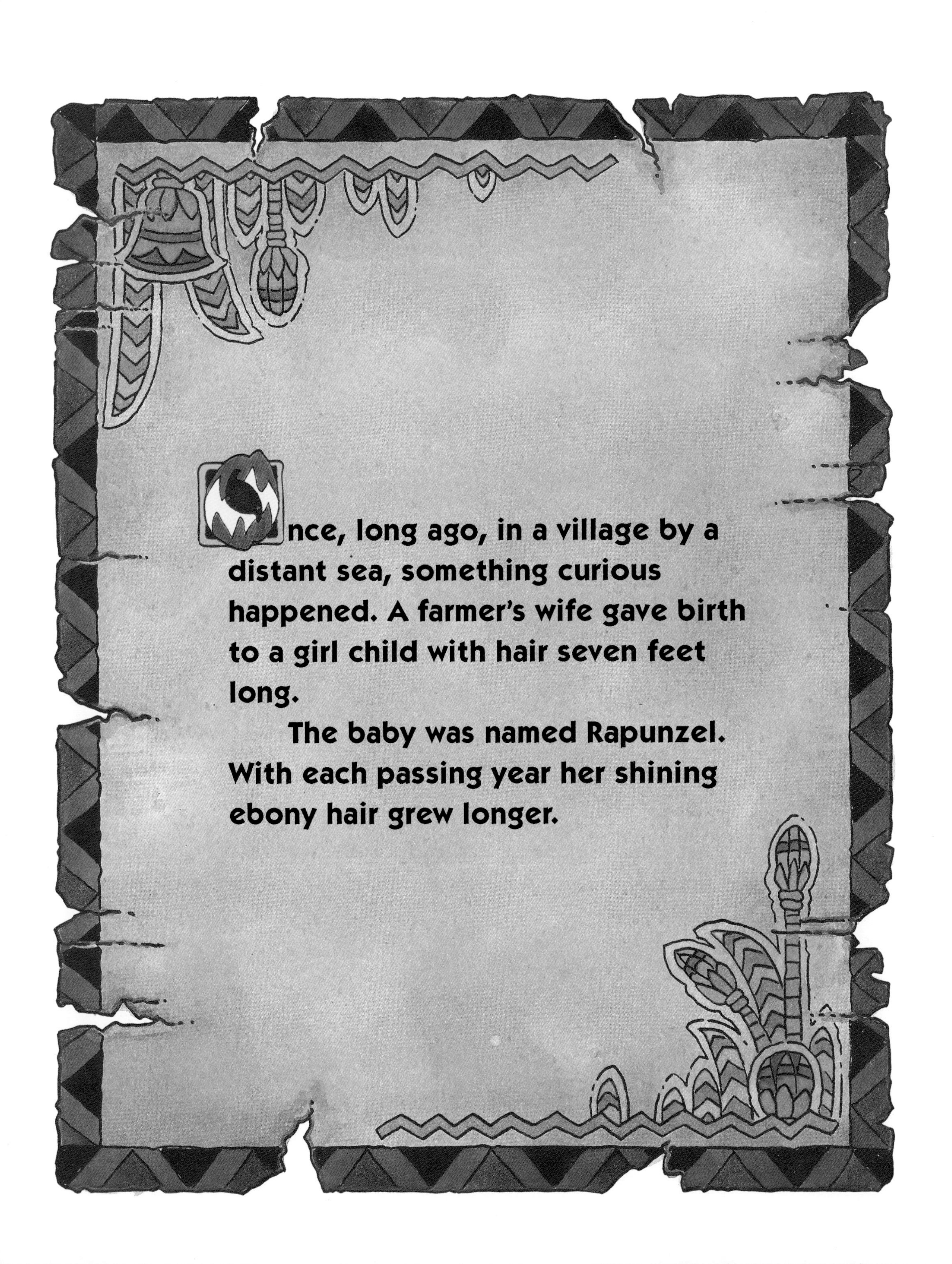

Once, long ago, in a village by a distant sea, something curious happened. A farmer's wife gave birth to a girl child with hair seven feet long.

The baby was named Rapunzel. With each passing year her shining ebony hair grew longer.

RAPUNZEL'S HAIR GREW LONGER

One day, not long after her seventh birthday, Rapunzel was watering the garden cabbage patch. As she worked she sang with a voice that sounded like silver bells and happy birds.

A sly old witch hobbled by and was enchanted with the beautiful voice. She decided to steal Rapunzel away and keep her for a companion.

The witch, with whispered magic words, cast a spell on Rapunzel and told her to follow into the dark jungle.

And her parents never saw her again.

THE WITCH CAST A MAGIC SPELL

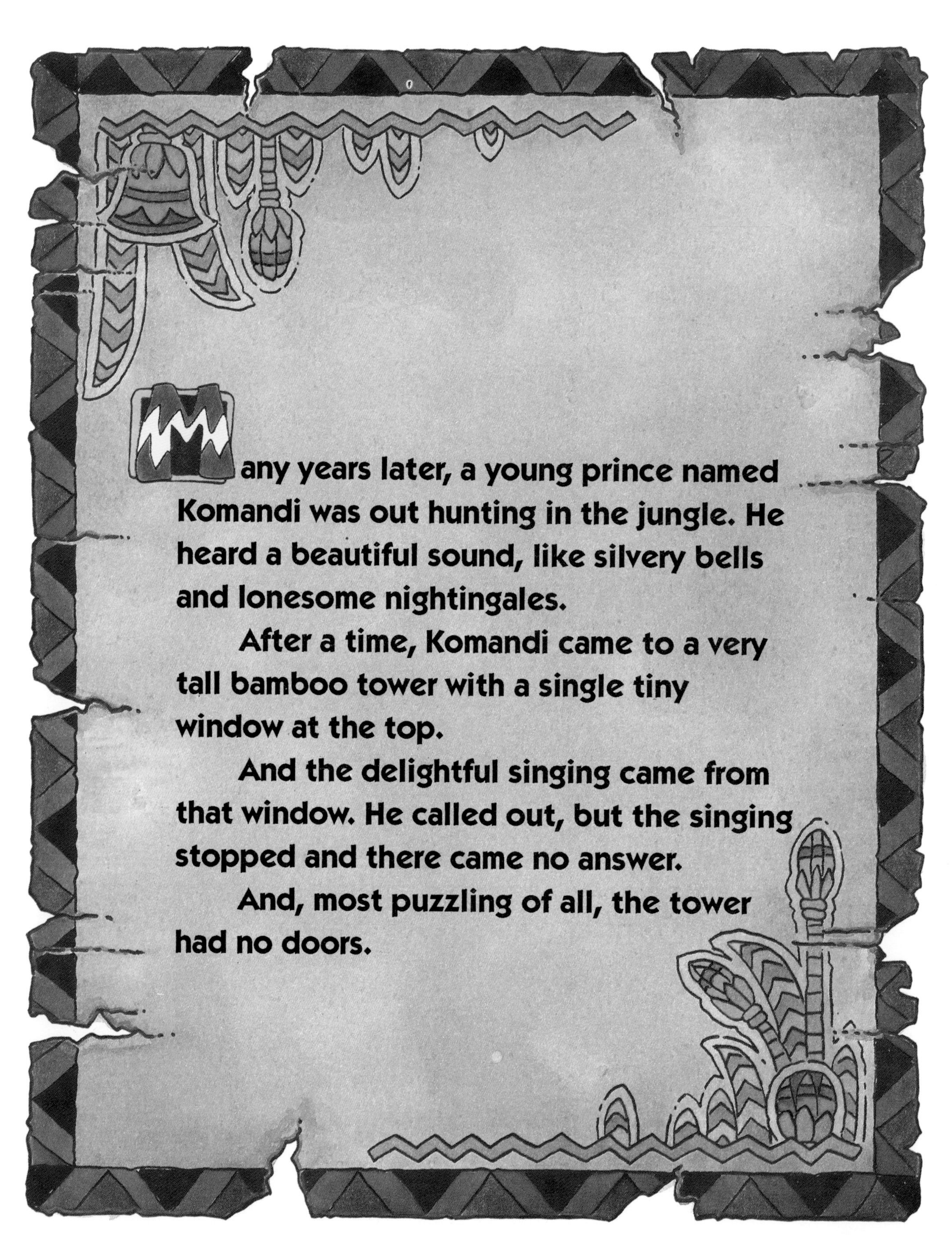

Many years later, a young prince named Komandi was out hunting in the jungle. He heard a beautiful sound, like silvery bells and lonesome nightingales.

After a time, Komandi came to a very tall bamboo tower with a single tiny window at the top.

And the delightful singing came from that window. He called out, but the singing stopped and there came no answer.

And, most puzzling of all, the tower had no doors.

THE PRINCE SAW A TOWER

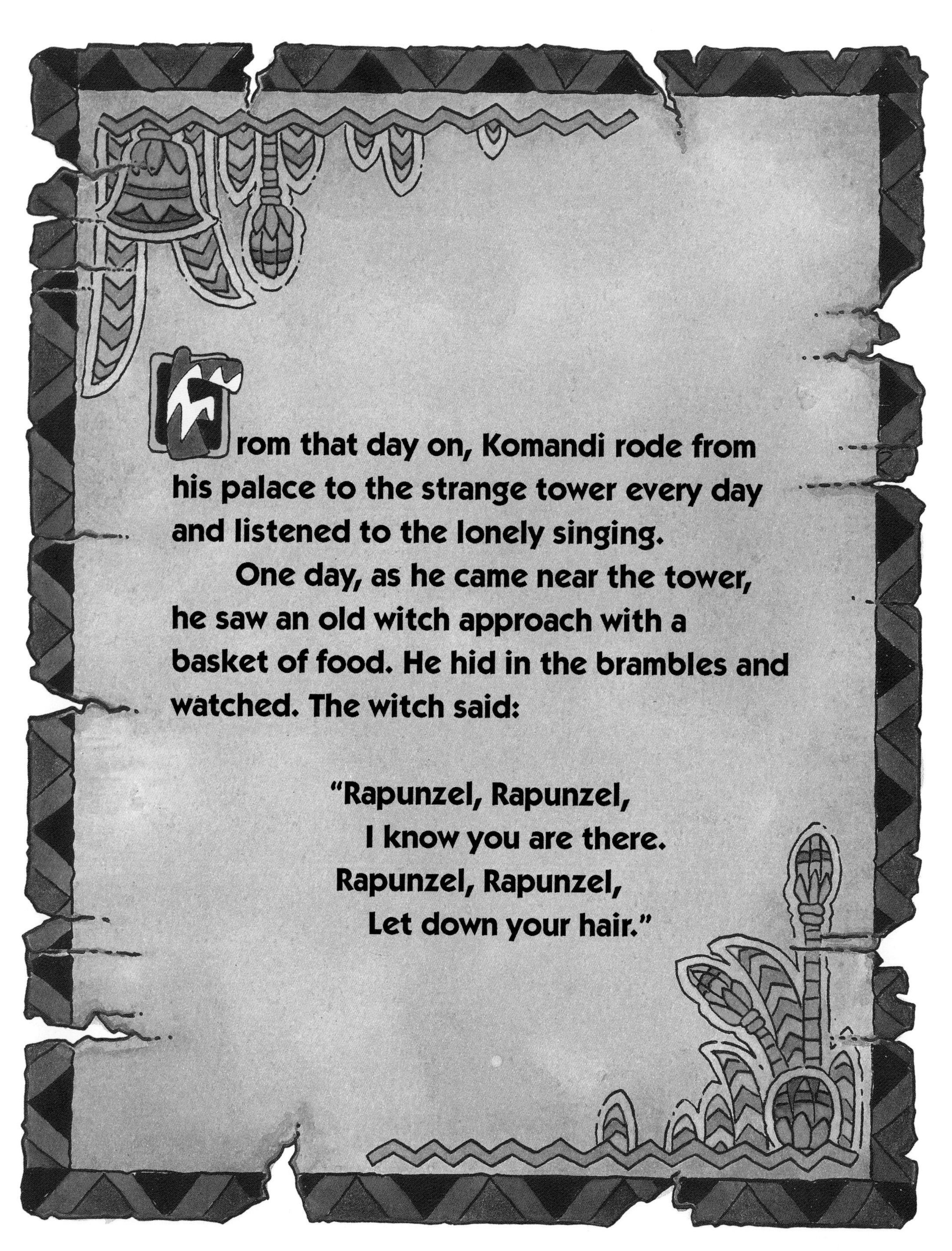

From that day on, Komandi rode from his palace to the strange tower every day and listened to the lonely singing.

One day, as he came near the tower, he saw an old witch approach with a basket of food. He hid in the brambles and watched. The witch said:

"Rapunzel, Rapunzel,
I know you are there.
Rapunzel, Rapunzel,
Let down your hair."

AN OLD WITCH CAME TO THE TOWER

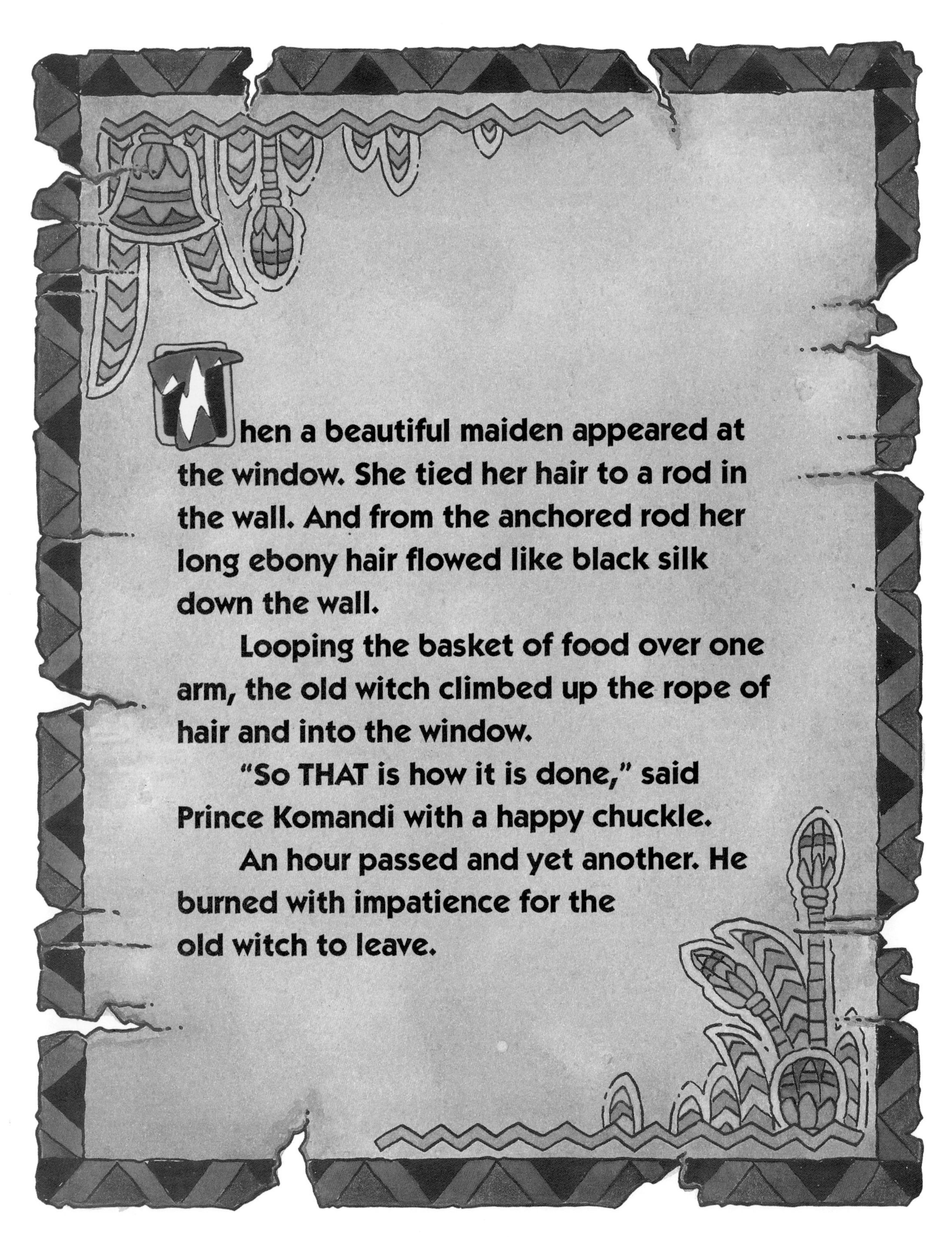

Then a beautiful maiden appeared at the window. She tied her hair to a rod in the wall. And from the anchored rod her long ebony hair flowed like black silk down the wall.

Looping the basket of food over one arm, the old witch climbed up the rope of hair and into the window.

"So THAT is how it is done," said Prince Komandi with a happy chuckle.

An hour passed and yet another. He burned with impatience for the old witch to leave.

SHE CLiMBED UP THE ROPE OF HAiR

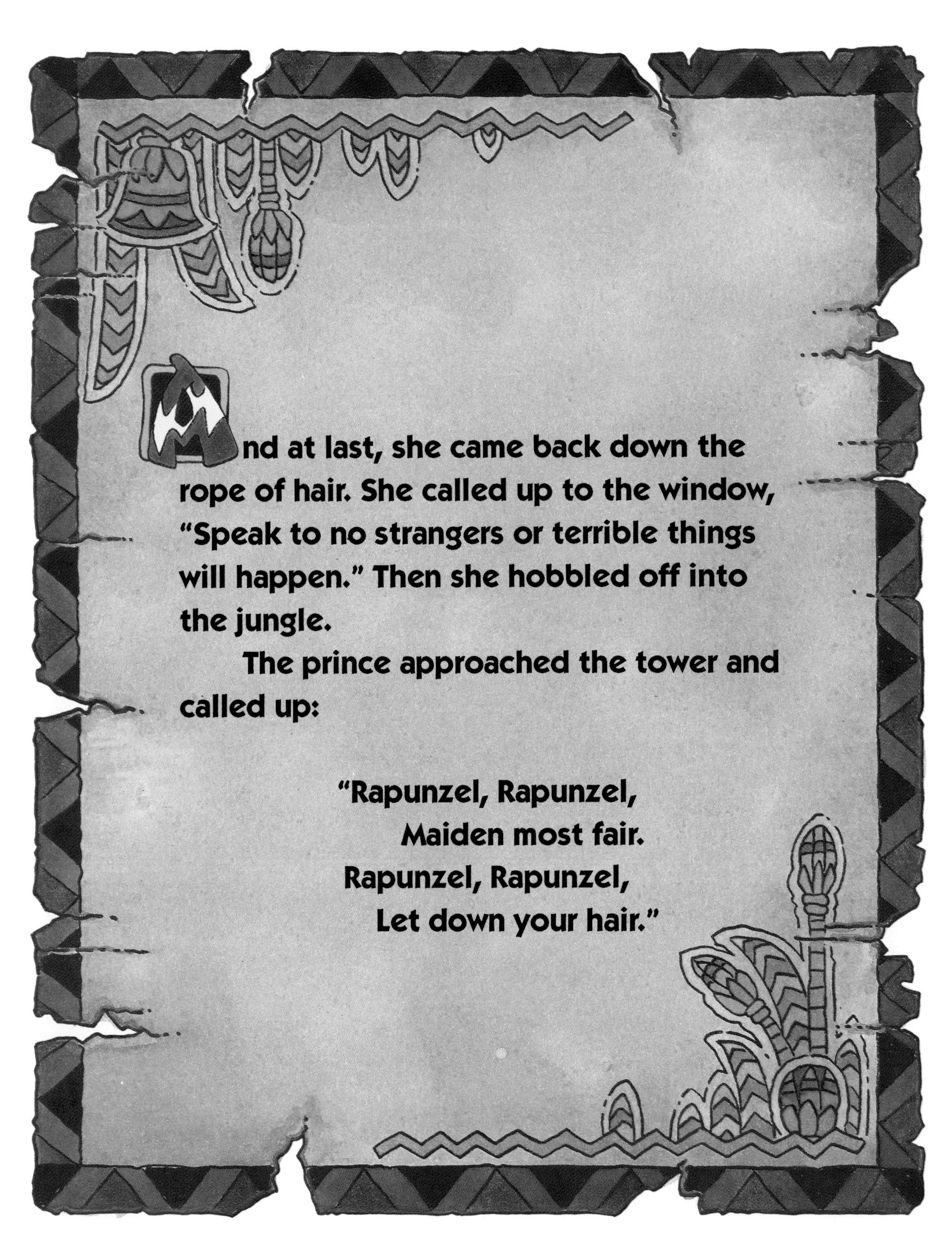

And at last, she came back down the rope of hair. She called up to the window, "Speak to no strangers or terrible things will happen." Then she hobbled off into the jungle.

The prince approached the tower and called up:

"Rapunzel, Rapunzel,
Maiden most fair.
Rapunzel, Rapunzel,
Let down your hair."

THE PRiNCE TRiED iT

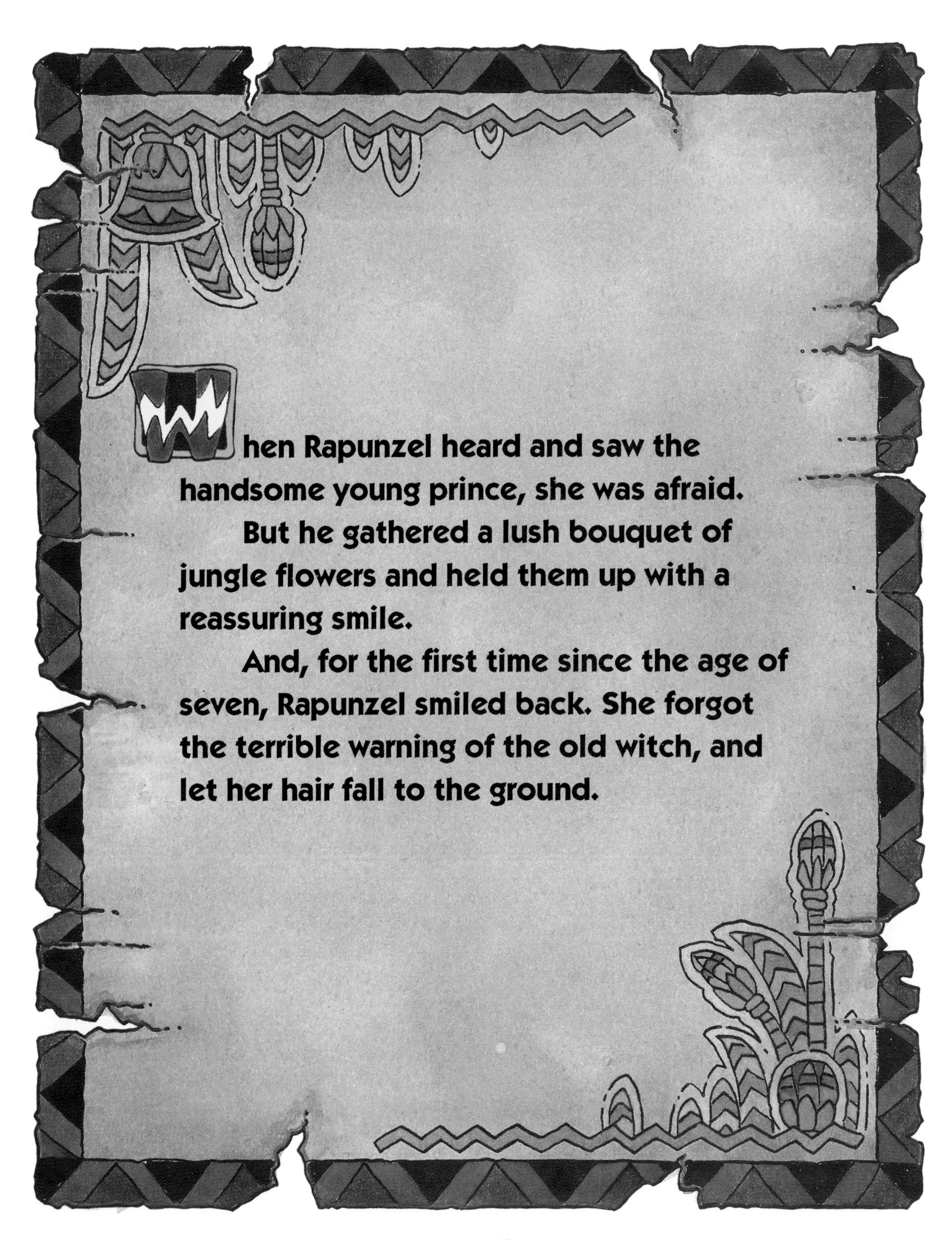

When Rapunzel heard and saw the handsome young prince, she was afraid.

But he gathered a lush bouquet of jungle flowers and held them up with a reassuring smile.

And, for the first time since the age of seven, Rapunzel smiled back. She forgot the terrible warning of the old witch, and let her hair fall to the ground.

RAPUNZEL WAS UNCERTAIN

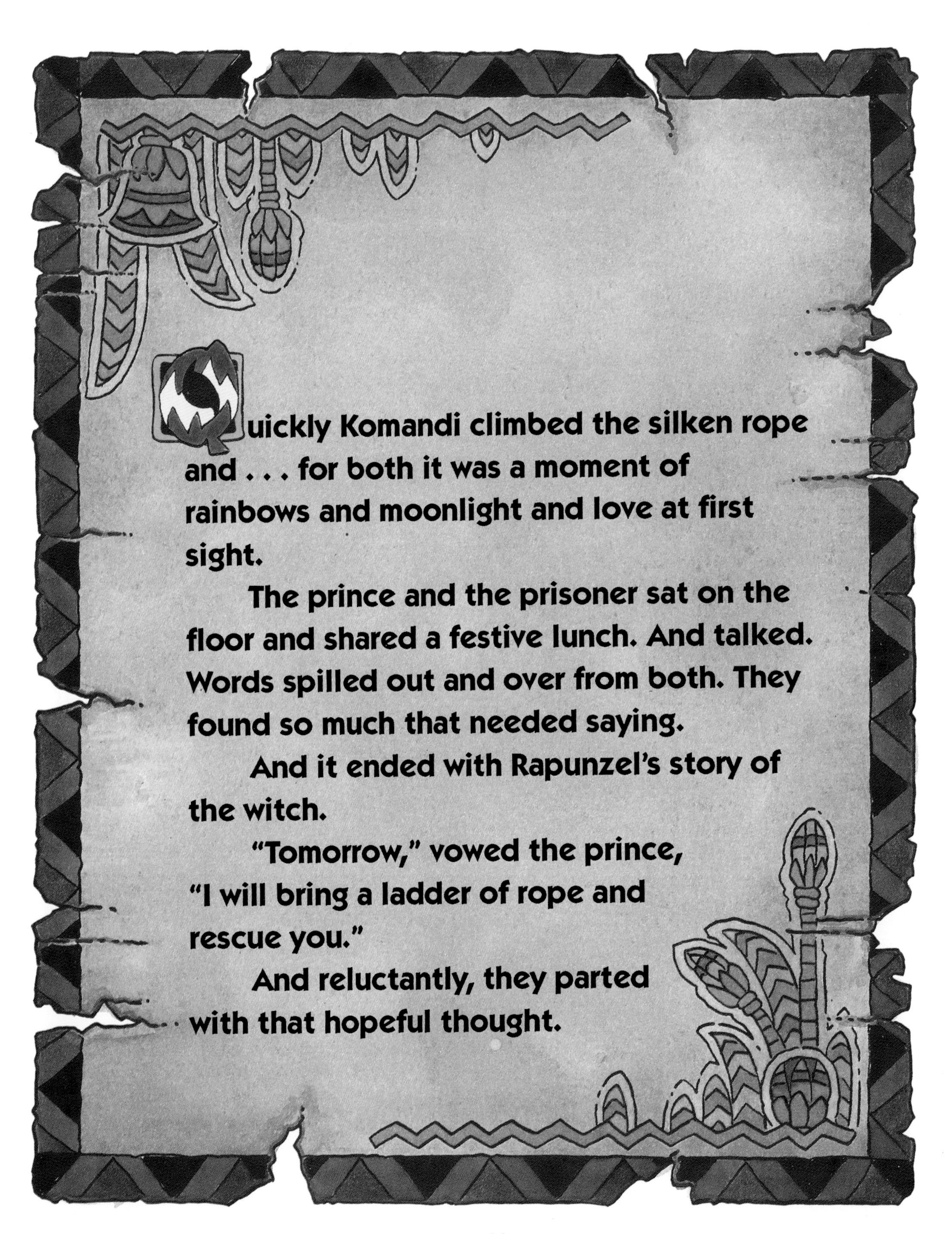

Quickly Komandi climbed the silken rope and . . . for both it was a moment of rainbows and moonlight and love at first sight.

The prince and the prisoner sat on the floor and shared a festive lunch. And talked. Words spilled out and over from both. They found so much that needed saying.

And it ended with Rapunzel's story of the witch.

"Tomorrow," vowed the prince, "I will bring a ladder of rope and rescue you."

And reluctantly, they parted with that hopeful thought.

LOVE AT FIRST SIGHT

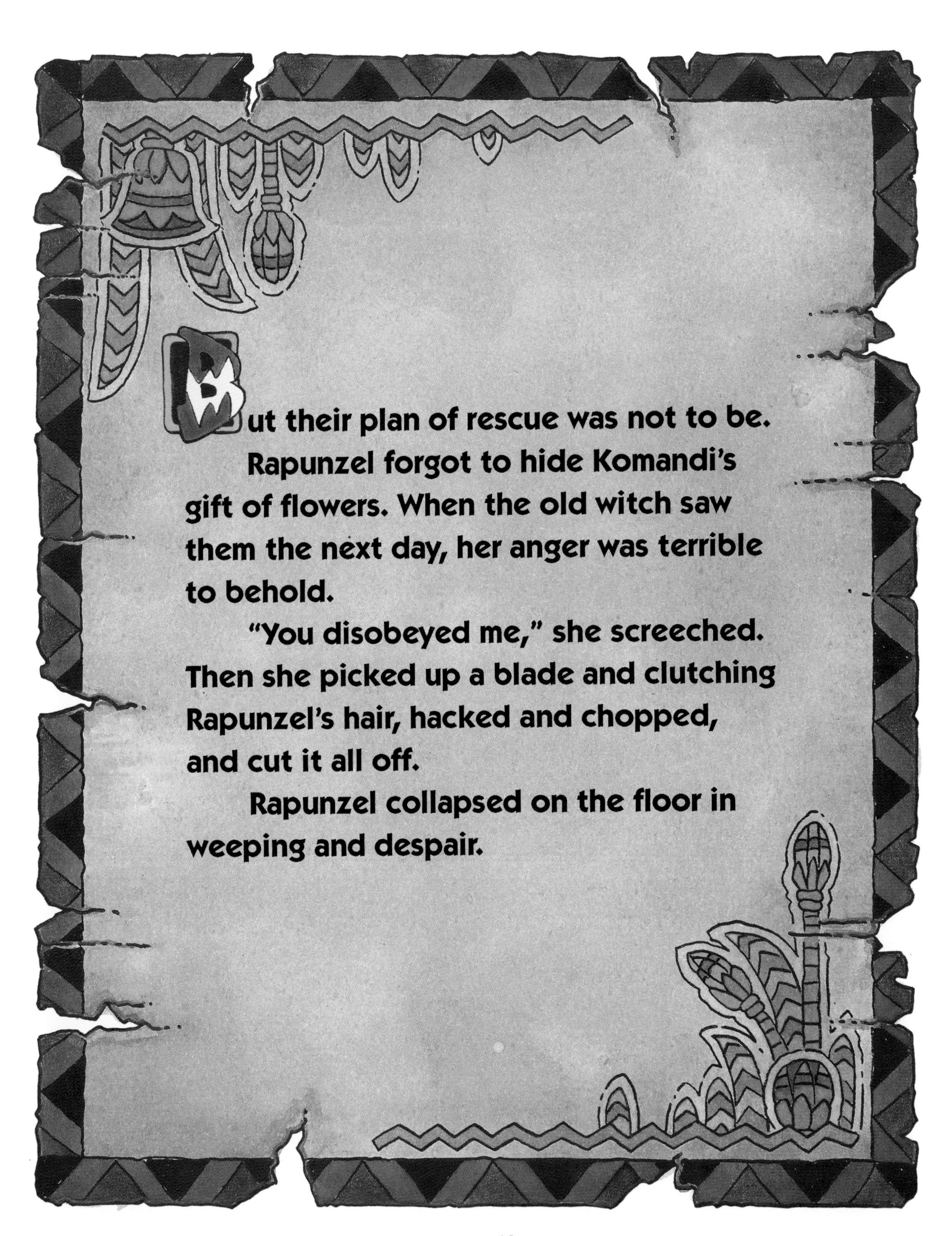

But their plan of rescue was not to be.

Rapunzel forgot to hide Komandi's gift of flowers. When the old witch saw them the next day, her anger was terrible to behold.

"You disobeyed me," she screeched. Then she picked up a blade and clutching Rapunzel's hair, hacked and chopped, and cut it all off.

Rapunzel collapsed on the floor in weeping and despair.

THE WITCH CUT OFF HER HAIR

Later that terrible day, Prince Komandi approached the tower. He called up:

"Rapunzel, Rapunzel,
Let down your hair.
We shall flee from the witch
Who keeps you up there."

The witch had tied Rapunzel's hair to the rod. Staying out of sight, she let the hair fall. She chuckled wickedly and sang softly:

"Steal my child
Away from me?
Well, bold prince,
We shall see! We shall see!"

THE WiTCH TRiCKED THE PRiNCE

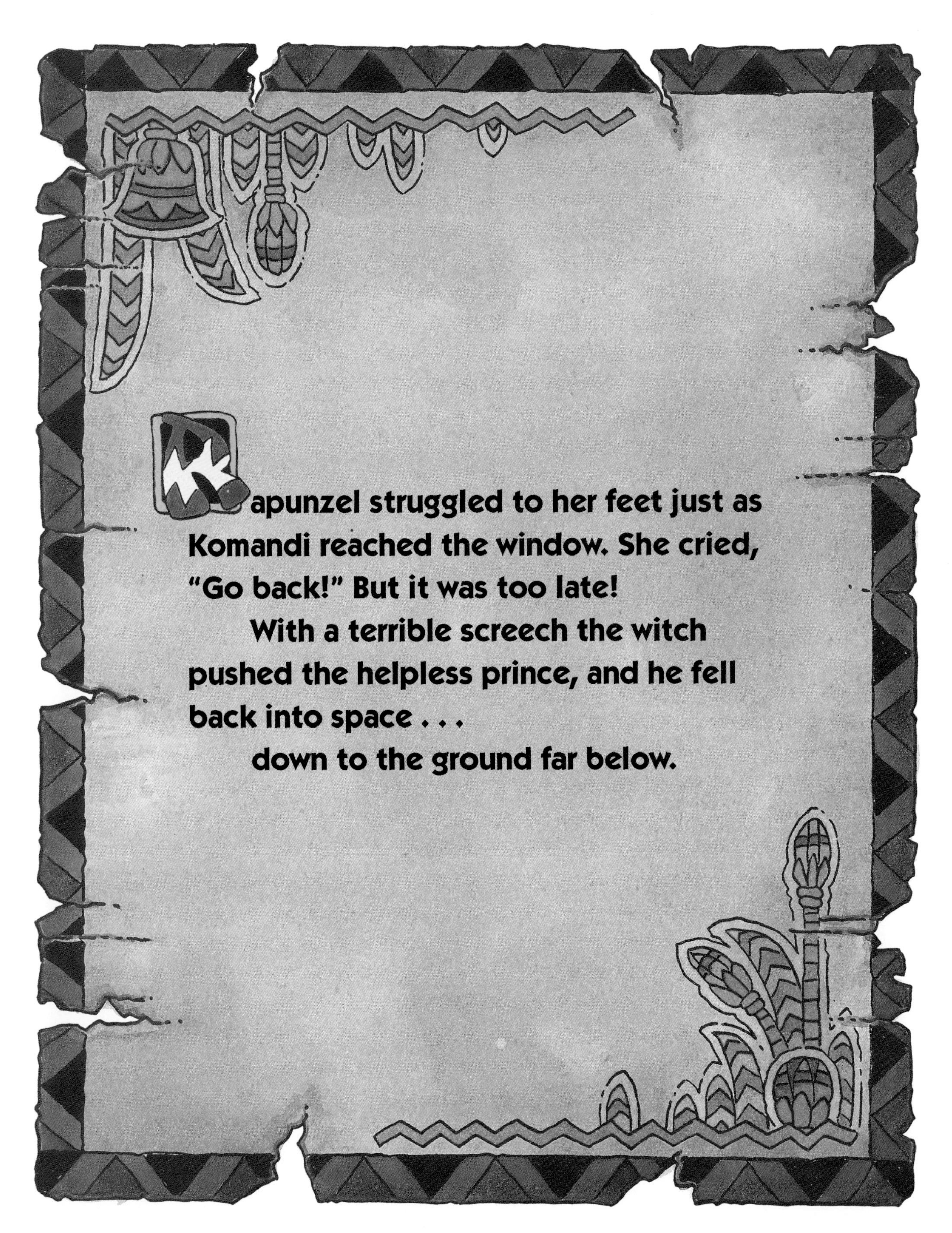

Rapunzel struggled to her feet just as Komandi reached the window. She cried, "Go back!" But it was too late!

With a terrible screech the witch pushed the helpless prince, and he fell back into space . . .

down to the ground far below.

THE WiTCH PUSHED THE PRiNCE

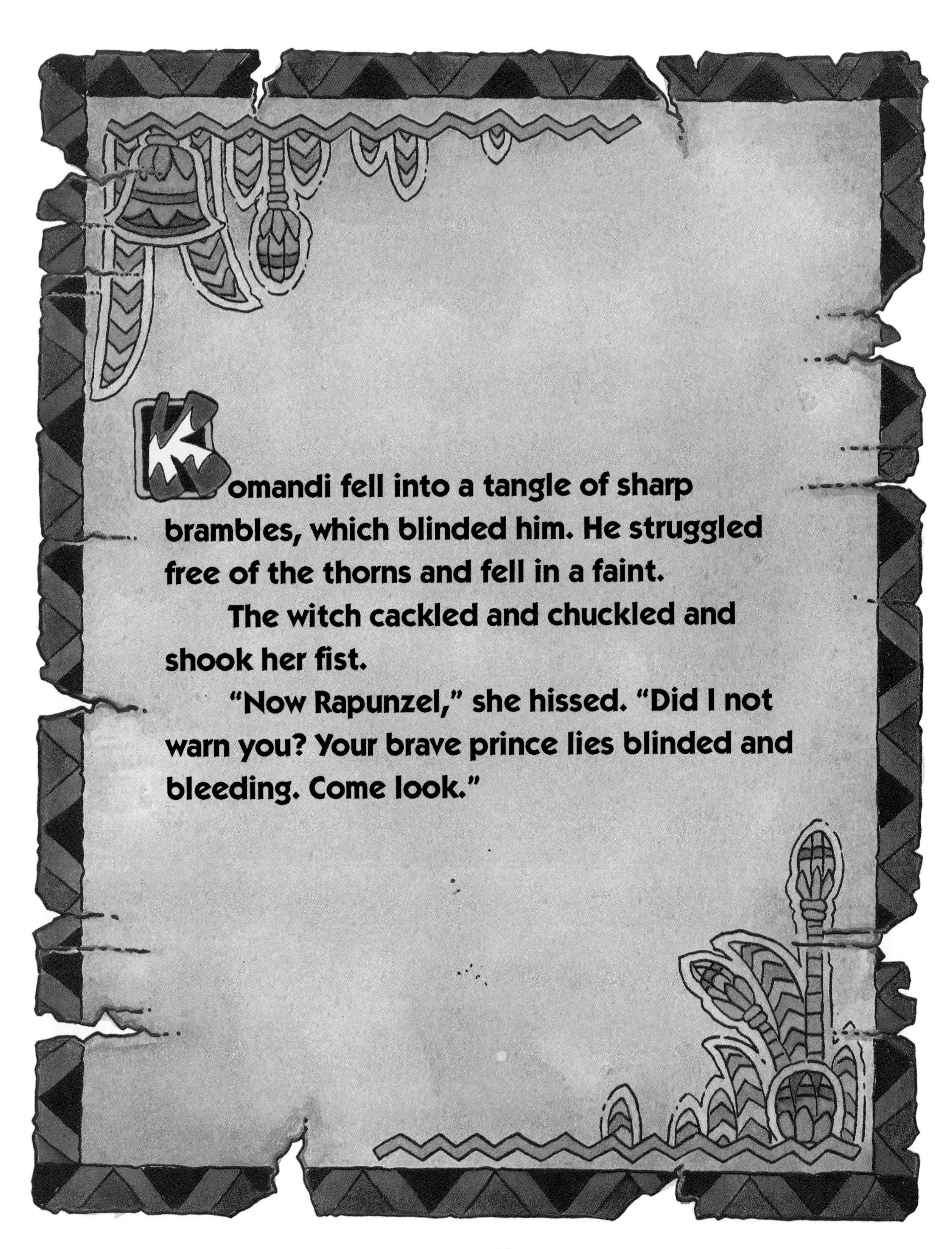

Komandi fell into a tangle of sharp brambles, which blinded him. He struggled free of the thorns and fell in a faint.

The witch cackled and chuckled and shook her fist.

"Now Rapunzel," she hissed. "Did I not warn you? Your brave prince lies blinded and bleeding. Come look."

THE THORNS BLINDED HIM

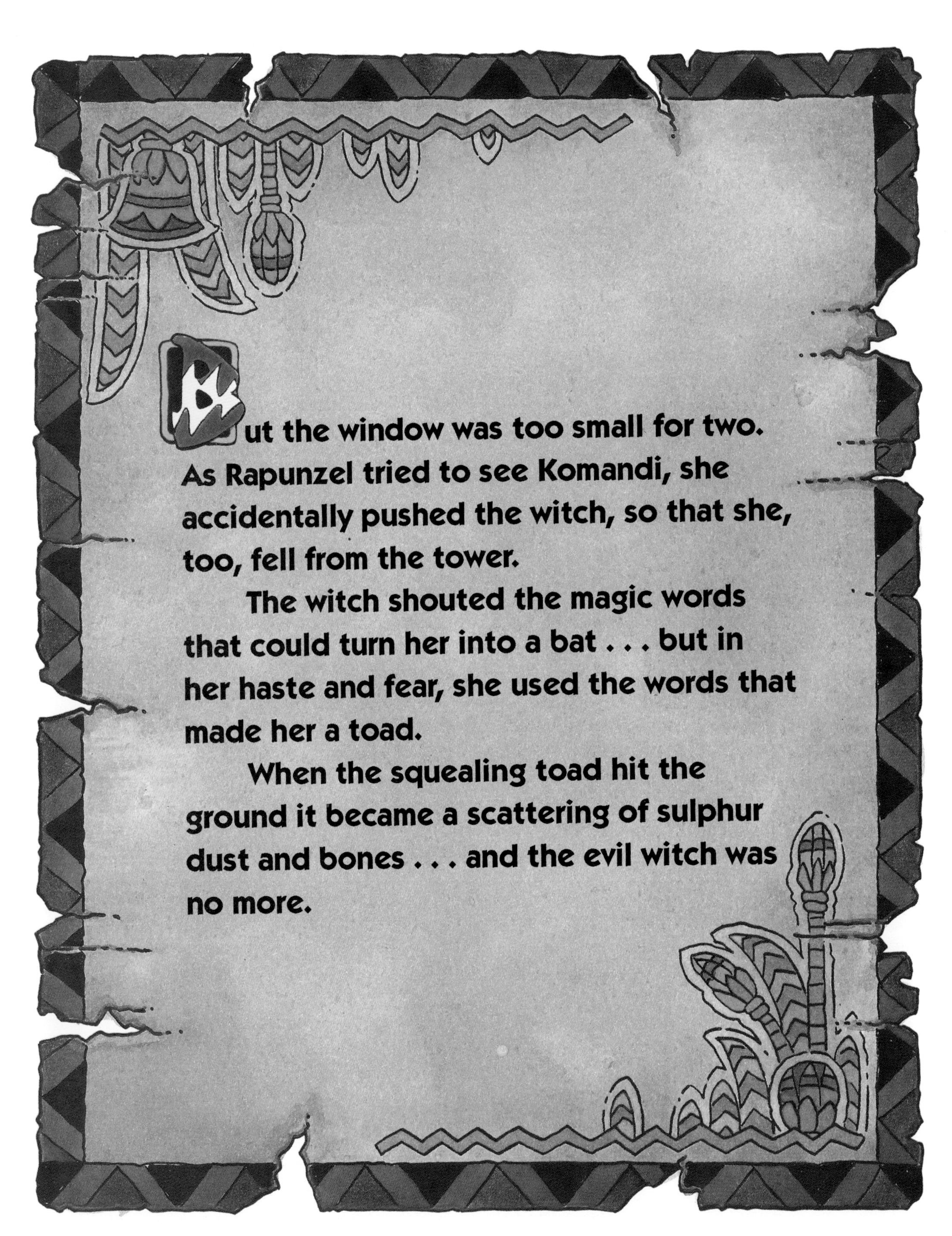

But the window was too small for two. As Rapunzel tried to see Komandi, she accidentally pushed the witch, so that she, too, fell from the tower.

The witch shouted the magic words that could turn her into a bat . . . but in her haste and fear, she used the words that made her a toad.

When the squealing toad hit the ground it became a scattering of sulphur dust and bones . . . and the evil witch was no more.

THE WITCH TURNED INTO A TOAD

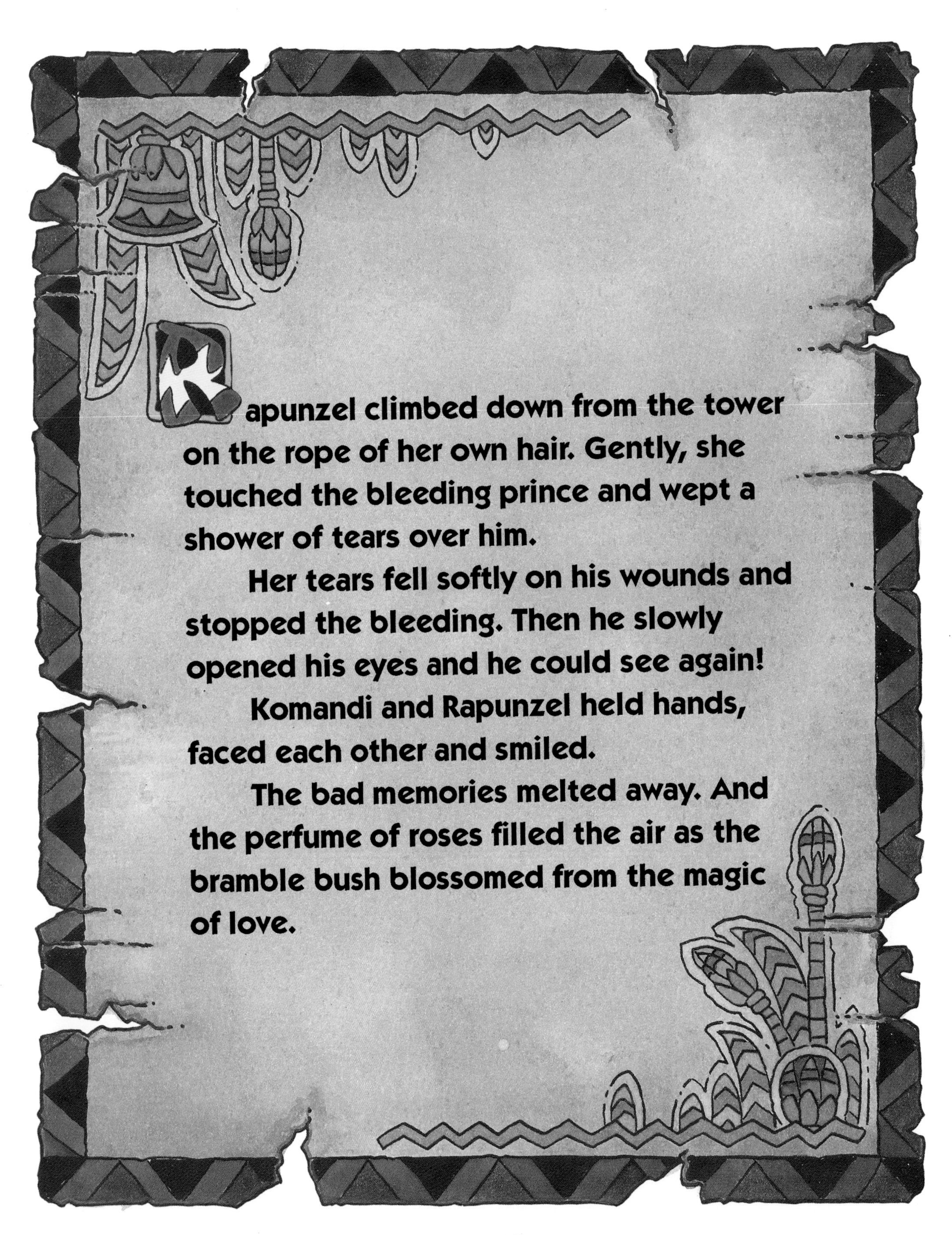

Rapunzel climbed down from the tower on the rope of her own hair. Gently, she touched the bleeding prince and wept a shower of tears over him.

Her tears fell softly on his wounds and stopped the bleeding. Then he slowly opened his eyes and he could see again!

Komandi and Rapunzel held hands, faced each other and smiled.

The bad memories melted away. And the perfume of roses filled the air as the bramble bush blossomed from the magic of love.

SUNSHINE AND MAGIC

When Komandi took Rapunzel to his palace for a life of days filled with sunshine and laughter, and she was never lonely again.